D0172279

Note to parents, carers and teachers

Read it yourself is a series of modern stories, favourite characters and traditional tales written in a simple way for children who are learning to read. The books can be read independently or as part of a guided reading session.

Each book is carefully structured to include many high-frequency words vital for first reading. The sentences on each page are supported closely by pictures to help with understanding, and to offer lively details to talk about.

The books are graded into four levels that progressively introduce wider vocabulary and longer stories as a reader's ability and confidence grows.

Ideas for use

- Ask how your child would like to approach reading at this stage. Would he prefer to hear you read the story first, or would he like to read the story to you and see how he gets on?
- Help him to sound out any words he does not know.
- Developing readers can be concentrating so hard on the words that they sometimes don't fully grasp the meaning of what they're reading. Answering the puzzle questions on pages 46 and 47 will help with understanding.

For more information and advice on Read it yourself and book banding, visit www.ladybird.com/readityourself

Book Band 8

Level 3 is ideal for children who are developing reading confidence and stamina, and who are eager to read longer stories with a wider vocabulary.

Special features:

Detailed pictures for added interest and discussion

Wider vocabulary, reinforced through repetition

Longer sentences

Simple story structure

Educational Consultant: Geraldine Taylor
Book Banding Consultant: Kate Ruttle

A catalogue record for this book is available from the British Library

First published by Ladybird Books Ltd 2013
80 Strand, London, WC2R 0RL
A Penguin Company

002

© Mind Candy Ltd. Moshi Monsters is a trademark of Mind Candy Ltd. All rights reserved.

This edition MMXV.

Ladybird, Read It Yourself and the Ladybird Logo are registered or
unregistered trademarks of Ladybird Books Limited.

All rights reserved. No part of this publication may be reproduced,
stored in a retrieval system, or transmitted in any form or by any means,
electronic, mechanical, photocopying, recording or otherwise,
without the prior consent of the copyright owner.

ISBN: 978-0-72329-377-4

Printed in China

Written by Ronne Randall
Illustrated by Lea Wade

One night in Monstro City, Furi and lots of other monsters were waiting to see the Roxstar Zack Binspin. They were waiting for the Scare Guitar tryouts, too.

NDERGROUND
ISCO
Scare Guitar
Tryouts
TODAY

Roary Scrawl came out.
"No one knows where Zack Binspin is," he said. "There will be no show, and there will be no Scare Guitar tryouts in Monstro City until we find him."

"No!" the monsters screamed. "We want the tryouts! Do something, Roary!"

"All right," Roary Scrawl said at last. "You can have the tryouts on Music Island instead of Monstro City."

"Yes!" the monsters screamed back at him.

UNDERGRO
DISC

Furi ran all the way to the Port and found a boat that was going to Music Island. But a lot of other monsters were waiting to get on!

USIC ISLAND

"I don't want to wait all night," Furi thought. "I see another boat that's going to Music Island. I can take that boat out there instead!"

"It's good to have you on the boat,"
said the captain.
Furi thought there was something
funny about the captain, but he
REALLY wanted to go to Music Island.

Furi asked the captain when they would get to Music Island.

"We'll be there in a while," said the captain, "but until then there are lots of other fun things to do instead!"

After a while, Furi asked again, “Are we at Music Island yet?”

“Not yet,” said the captain. “We have time to go water skiing first!”

“I can’t water ski!” said Furi.

“Come on, it’s fun!” said the captain.

But water skiing was REALLY not fun for Furi. He just felt sick!

"I feel really sick," said Furi, when he got back on the boat. The captain was having fun, but all Furi wanted to do was get to Music Island!

At last, they came to Music Island.

"Music Island looks just as good as I thought it would," said Furi. "There's so much going on!"

There was a lot to see on Music Island. Most of all, the captain wanted to go to the fair.

"The fair looks so much fun!" Furi said to the captain.

ISLAND

Furi really liked the fair.
He won gifts for all his friends.
The captain won some gifts, too.

After the fair, Furi and the captain went to the Sandy Drain Hotel, where the captain was going to stay.
"It's funny that the captain is staying at the hotel," thought Furi.
"I thought it was just for stars!"

SANDY DRAIN
Hotel

Suddenly, the captain said, "It's time for the Scare Guitar tryouts!"

Furi ran all the way there and the captain came, too.

SCARE GUITAR
Tryouts

But there was no one at the tryouts. “Where are all the other monsters I saw at the Port?” Furi asked.

“I don’t know,” said the captain.

"It looks like the boat with the other monsters on didn't get here," said the captain. "But if there are no tryouts tonight, we can go back to the hotel instead."

"All right," said Furi.

There were lots of Roxstars with guitars staying at the hotel, and the captain went up to sing with them. They were all his friends!

"That's funny," thought Furi.

Suddenly, Furi saw that the captain was really Zack Binspin! He had just wanted to get away from Monstro City for a while and have some fun! Now he was singing just for Furi.

“I really had fun tonight,” Furi thought after the show. “There were no Scare Guitar tryouts, but I found Zack Binspin and I heard him sing – with real guitars! YES!”

How much do you remember about the story of Moshi Monsters: Furi on Music Island? Answer these questions and find out!

- Who are the monsters all waiting to see at the beginning of the story?
- Where do the Scare Guitar tryouts get moved to?
- What sport does the captain make Furi do while they're on the boat?
- Where do they go when they first get to Music Island?
- Where on Music Island is the captain staying?
- Who is the captain really?

Look at the different story sentences and match them to the characters who said them.

"We want the tryouts! Do something, Roary!"

"Music Island looks just as good as I thought it would."

"It's good to have you on the boat."

"There will be no show, and there will be no Scare Guitar tryouts in Monstro City until we find him."

Read it yourself with Ladybird

Tick the books you've read!

For more confident readers who can read simple stories with help.

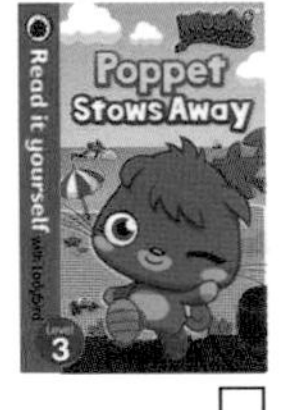

Longer stories for more independent, fluent readers.

The Read it yourself with Ladybird app is now available for iPad, iPhone and iPod touch

App also available on Android devices